more praise for

A LOVE LETTER

"In *A Love Letter*, lyrical vignettes place witness pinnacle as the speaker both chronicles and begets introspection. We observe cyclical mourning and cyclical hope. In these pages, we gather empathy as a cure for our human condition, with passages like, 'this journey is eminently finite and someone's departure can seem abrupt if you miss as little as a day, week or month.' Praise this work that allows us to look into another's eyes and see something beautiful"

DANIEL B. SUMMERHILL
Monterey County Poet Laureate
author of *Divine, Divine, Divine* and *Mausoleum of Flowers*

"Carmen's exquisite memoriam moves between the harshness of loss and ways in which our bodies accept its inevitability. It snapshots a personal moment with such beautiful transcendence that it draws in all the senses and will serve as lastly a guide to anyone else who has to later turn the pages of their own scrapbooks... I am forever changed."

TSHAKA CAMPBELL
Santa Clara County Poet Laureate
author of *Tunnel Vision, Muted Whispers*, and more

"As a person who witnessed two loved ones' minds sail away before their bodies departed, I can assure you that Carmen Kennedy has captured a maelstrom of emotions and delicately drew them onto the spathe of a calla lily. This profound prosimetrum captures the rememory of loss in a sequence of window panes all shattering with the sorrow, doubt, and the tenderest moments of humans coming together to hold one another up when the world seems like it is drifting away. Carmen captured the stages of grief in stained-glass. This is one of the most delicate works I have read in a long time—but the carefulness of how it was written relays the strength of the writer into the minds of those who read it—especially those who find pieces of themselves in the elegant layering of these pastel paned moments. This is a declaration of healing."

VERNON KEEVE III (TREY)
author of *Southern Migrant Mixtape*
education researcher at Columbia University

"Carmen Kennedy has written a poignant and rapturous tale of caregiving, grieving, and persevering. Her prose will grab you—let it."

SELENA ANDERSON
educator, writer
Rona Jaffe Award recipient

"This tenderly woven love letter will excavate memory of life's end with unexpected beginnings. Watching a once so alive stylish personality retreat into unknown territories, you seize this uncharted landscape and commit to it out of love, family, and duty. This love letter is an exquisite exercise on how to charter mental and emotional scenes staged with a cast of characters that add melancholy and humor to life's play. You're about to take a journey following a roadmap on how to acclimatize yourself while a loved one gradually ceases to know you, themselves, or their body. This letter of love will assist you in navigating the most intrinsic elements of caregiving and the difficulty of letting go. This tome will be of great value and benefit to many."

TUREEDA MIKELL
author of *Synchronicity: The Oracle of Sun Medicine*,
and curator of *Patrice Lumumba: An Anthology of Writers on Black Liberation*

"Carmen Kennedy's essay collection is a clear-eyed, incisive, important contribution to an emerging public sphere dialogue around medical racism, the systemic 'bad medicine' that too often impairs the lives of our loved ones—in this case, the multi-generational members of the author's own family."

KEENAN NORRIS
educator
author of *Chi Boy: Native Sons and Chicago Reckonings*,
The Confession of Copeland Cane, and more

NOMADIC PRESS

OAKLAND
PHILADELPHIA
XALAPA

WWW.NOMADICPRESS.ORG

MISSON STATEMENT Through publications, events, and active community participation, Nomadic Press collectively weaves together platforms for intentionally marginalized voices to take their rightful place within the world of the written and spoken word. Through our limited means, we are simply attempting to help right the centuries' old violence and silencing that should never have occurred in the first place and build alliances and community partnerships with others who share a collective vision for a future far better than today.

INVITATIONS Nomadic Press wholeheartedly accepts invitations to read your work during our open reading period every year. To learn more or to extend an invitation, please visit: www.nomadicpress.org/invitations

DISTRIBUTION
Orders by teachers, libraries, trade bookstores, or wholesalers:

Nomadic Press Distribution
orders@nomadicpress.org
(510) 500-5162

Small Press Distribution
spd@spdbooks.org
(510) 524-1668 / (800) 869-7553

A Love Letter

This book was made possible by a loving community of chosen family and friends, old and new. For author questions or to book a reading at your bookstore, university/school, or alternative establishment, please send an email to info@nomadicpress.org.

Cover art and author portrait by Arthur Johnstone

Published by Nomadic Press, 1941 Jackson Street, Suite 20, Oakland, CA 94612
First printing, 2023

Library of Congress Cataloging-in-Publication Data

Title: ***A Love Letter***
p. cm.
Summary: *A Love Letter* has the power to speak outside of time (or through time) as did my beloved aunt who left a paper trail that evidenced she kept me in her thoughts. She'd drafted an Advance Directive, and purchased some modest burial insurance, and protected a few memories that might have otherwise been forgotten. A love letter became how she chose to say goodbye and go with grace. So, I wish in many ways to reciprocate her love with this little book—a re-memory—reflecting where I was when she left this world, and where I am now, and where in the future any one of us might be.

[1. **FAMILY & RELATIONSHIPS** / Death, Grief, Bereavement. 2. **FAMILY & RELATIONSHIPS** / Family History & Genealogy. 3. **FICTION** / African American & Black / Women. 4. **FICTION** / Family Life / General.]

LIBRARY OF CONGRESS CONTROL NUMBER: 2022947173
ISBN: 978-1-955239-44-8

A LOVE LETTER

A LOVE LETTER

CARMEN KENNEDY

NOMADIC
PRESS

Oakland · Philadelphia · Xalapa

CONTENTS

INTRODUCTION

I've mostly kept the guilt that followed me up to and after the day my aunt entered the home, to myself and the notes that eventually turned into the narrative resting on these pages, glib ruminations on the humanity I found in the Alzheimer's wing of a Campbell, California nursing home. It was my first encounter with neurodegenerative diseases, specifically Alzheimer's, and it was the first time I'd dealt with institutions that served patients with dementia: people who I've chosen to name quite differently in this recollection and whose stories I have re-woven into memories that are bound to someday disappear.

INTROSPECTION:

I wanted to be careful about mischaracterizing what I'd witnessed at the nursing home as trauma. It didn't fit what people associate with the level of harm we'd often associate with trauma: the clap of gunshot, the threat of violence, assault, terror; no, what I recall about the disease and the institution was far from these but nevertheless jarring. There was something quintessentially horrific about the way dementia consumed identities, memories, and everything that tethered a person to purpose, and people, and joy. I feared its isolation, the mental and physical state in which it trapped its victims, like a purgatory of sorts that dared me to engage the souls it ensnared. So, I found myself braving my racing heart on the lead up to each nursing home visit and fighting depression with each goodbye.

IMPETUS:

I'm inspired as more narratives of people long silenced by the documented world appear in creative nonfiction and other genres. Boundaries are blurring between art (pure expression) and anthropology (researching myths of humanity and the origins of humankind). I believe the narrative synthesis of the two allows artists like me to not only illustrate time, place, and setting, but the thoughts and feelings of characters; and specifically with nonfiction, the thoughts, feelings, and experiences of real people. In fact, my impetus for using a mix of narrative, prose, and verse has been to explore language, and complicated characters, and truths with potential to lead us to clearer historical and contemporary understandings.

IMPACT:

I wanted to address this impetus with *A Love Letter*, lending my unvarnished lens, in the spirit of critics like Stuart Hall, activists like Sonia Sanchez, and scholars like Harriet A. Washington whose work I admire and see as essential to any discussion on well-being. I also wanted to contextualize institutionalized, long-term, or palliative care, ostensibly one in the same. These are systems predestined to profit off an infinite supply of the old and infirmed. They are hardwired to be self-sustaining and detrimental to ecosystems of patients, families, and caregivers. They use reductionist tactics that dehumanize and target individuals for profit based on age, health, economics, and implicitly, race. *A Love Letter* is therefore where I write back to all this by recording a few personal moments in the daily lives of some of the real people these systems consume. *A Love Letter* should make you feel uncomfortable while it inspires your active support for newly imagined forms of universal, comprehensive, care that's free for all of us.

THE END

After being groomed by a nursing home attendant, she drew in all four limbs and lay there rigid like a pill-bug protecting its middle. Her dark pupils bore into me as if some obdurate part of her could excavate my thoughts. I told myself, you're letting her in your head. *You're imagining improbabilities from a mind, lost in an interminable void and inaccessible beyond these contortions.*

The hospice nurses seemed to float around her with the solemnity of spirits who could intuit from her labored breath something other than the end simply struggling to begin. I watched them hover and speak sotto voce about things they thought she might want if she were able to voice her desire for anything, if her tongue had not been tied by the disease.

I had imagined, or perhaps really hoped, the irony of Alzheimer's had wiped away this moment, as it had wiped away all the things that once weighed upon her; the marriages that long ago dissolved like the antacids she had taken to stomach them; a decade that waxed in '82 with the news her first-born had acquired the immunodeficiency and waned with his burial and news her second-born's fate would be the same. I had really hoped she'd forgotten how their skin bruised like ripened plums until receding, drawing close to their bones as would dried fruit around its pit. I'd hoped she'd forgotten the tiny, rock-hard thing of the same size taking root in her bosom and feeding where her sons once grew fat. And I'd hoped she had forgotten sitting in Oncology, sipping poison-cocktails, lamenting her losses and the crown of tightly wound silver curls that sloughed off her head.

I'm hoping these terribly marked memories were wiped away with all the thoughts she might have otherwise let roam 'round in her head; a loved one's disposition at any given time; an unexpected kindness; an embarrassment; a foible; a future, vanquished the day she was diagnosed.

THE BODY BEFORE

It seems almost impossible to paint a clear picture of my aunt in her last days and hours, as earlier versions of her come to mind, versions of her, full of life. She was funny and sprite. She was propelled by a bit of useful obsessive-compulsiveness which meant her home was always immaculate; her hair, coiffed; her make-up, fresh; and her wardrobe, impeccable.

She made up for what she lacked in quantity with quality; that is, she had a knack for styling the hand-me-downs gifted to her by her mother's employer. She breathed new life into ivy-league pullovers and gently worn Pendletons, and the care she took with these modest things taught me to recognize good value, especially my own.

Alzheimer's would however have her abandon the effort she once put into everything, including herself. Her perfectly pinned curls were supplanted with wild, grizzled wisps; her classic style, with a diaper and housecoat; her cares, with the encroachment of plaque and neurofibrillary tangles.

My self-assured aunt who had single-mindedly lived her life up to that point was lost. And when it came time for me to care for her, she was thoroughly dependent; when she became my responsibility, she had needs that far exceeded what I could manage on my own.

Dementia was something I'm sure she had never thought of in the years before she'd planned her retirement, nor had she thought of the possibility of being hit with it in the years beyond that. Nevertheless she was.

And when she decided to draft her Advance Directive, she couldn't have imagined Alzheimer's would be equally if not more formidable than the thing that had taken her sons. So, her Advance Directive was a love letter of sorts, an absolution she had thoughtfully secured in the aftermath of AIDS. And it spared me some of the same mortal decisions she faced: when to apply medicine and hope and when to let go and let God.

My guilt sounded loudest in a cacophony of inner voices the day I left her to the nursing home staff. It was unbearable, even as I knew the decision had come after months of wringing my hands, weighing my options, and watching her sundown on consecutive nights, worrying if she would reach across the stove again in an attempt to rinse her hands with the blue flames, or tip into the living room to confuse the chaise bergère for the bathroom commode. It eventually became impossible to fully "adult"-proof her world as she had turned to fishing hallucinations from a bucket of ammonia and water I thought I had judiciously hidden away.

THE MIXED BLESSING

Amberwood Gardens was not the first nursing home I'd visited, but it was the last. And although this is something I'd like to think the friendly staff and the smell of its shampooed carpet influenced, it wasn't, at least not to the same extent of my sheer exhaustion. I was simply tired, and as such, surrendered, signing my aunt's pension away in what seemed like an act of desperation.

Sometime shortly after I'd secured my aunt's room and weathered the transition, I started to question the system into which I'd placed her, partly based on the facility's high costs–these had me seeing red–and partly because I felt I was without options. Eldercare had a monopoly on aging in a world where everyone grows old.

I'd like to think if my aunt had been able, she would have assured me, saying, "The Lord led you here in an emergency, so count your blessings and get on with it." Amberwood Gardens was perhaps a blessing but it felt more like a dispensation that would eventually cost our family its generational wealth.

The Amberwood facility was in San Jose. It was off a major highway, one block west of a well-worn avenue straddled by suburbia and a few gentrified malls, And it was thankfully not far from my home. It was staffed with people I truly believed could make my aunt's last years better than they might have been were she with me. The cleanliness of the Amberwood lounges and corridors were unrivaled by peer homes in the area, but nevertheless it was a nursing home, a last resort.

I was pinch-hitting on my way to finding a more sustainable, long-term care solution. I tried to manage late nights sitting up with my aunt and early mornings when I had to muster the strength to get through another day. Both late and early situations were proving our "at-home" effort simply could not last. So, I devoted every thankful pause in my day to desperate internet searches, and these led me to adult daycare facilities.

I learned to appreciate the fact that daycare was like childcare in that the staff engaged attendees apropos to their level of ability. But while most of the attendees were high functioning, my aunt was not. In the beginning I figured this wouldn't be much of a problem, after all, none of the attendees had come to daycare to engage in deep conversation or find a chess partner.

I signed the enrollment form which basically read,

'*will provide a snack and ensure attendees are safe*; and,

'*will occasionally make eye contact with attendees and smile*'
(although neither of these were actually in writing).

And, wanting to see daycare as a solution, I chose to overlook the fine print.

'*will assist attendees with toileting, but not with soiled clothing or pull-ups.*'

And of course everything soils over time.

The day I decided to dress her in a pair of nice wool slacks and light-weight sweater placketted with grosgrain, they called to apologize about the blowout. I think the woman on the phone was trying to be discreet, saying, "Your aunt had a little accident," a statement seriously undercutting the severity of what had happened.

In fact, she had put it so delicately, I was convinced I simply had to appear with a change of clothes, clean things up, and be on my way. However, this was not the case. The quote unquote accident had traveled down my aunt's pant leg and into her shoe.

It was 2014 and the median cost of adult daycare was $77
per hour,
too exorbitant for a snack, safe surroundings,
and smiles from one or two attendants with little else.

The cost of care and the advanced stage of the disease made daycare and its counterpart, residential care, terribly inaccessible long-term. Neither daycare nor residential care accepted MediCal, the California state program that's meant to supplement the cost of care for those of us who can barely afford it. But Amberwood happened to be a nursing home that accepted MediCal. California's annual median cost for a nursing home at that time was about $125,000. This cost necessitated MediCal then, as it necessitates it now. In fact, MediCal would better serve patients if it were to become a perennially accessible source of funding.

Everything my aunt had, pension, social security, and meager savings were paid to the home. MediCal would make up the difference and the state would recoup its disbursements with a lien (in the case of my aunt, a lien was placed on her nonexistent estate) meaning the state of California would seize every asset, from the smallest of things like a credit card rebate, to the largest, like insurance proceeds.

Nursing homes have the capacity to leverage a system of
guaranteed payment,
guaranteed patients,

and the guarantee that families, with little or no resources, will sign-up for a moment's rest.

The system seems unfair,
especially if you believe nursing home care to be
an extension of healthcare and healthcare to be a human right.

DEDICATION AND DUTY

The Amberwood Gardens Sales Representative was dedicated to her job. She knew all the right places to pause, "Your aunt will feel at home here," and all the right places to push, "Our staff and our facility is equipped to provide 24-hour care that families just can't match."

She was right.

The nursing home was better.

She handed me a napkin awash in pastels and I looked at it, wondering if this was where she expected me to collapse in a puddle of tears. The napkin would have done quite well, had I any tears to shed, but I didn't. So, I sat there, curiously fixated on the representative's soft skills she surreptitiously used to offset her hard sell.

Nothing says "sign here" like freshly baked cookies; and in what could only be described as a sales office coup d'état, she handed me snickerdoodles tucked in another napkin. "Thanks," I said, welcoming their sweet cinnamon smell. There was no way out for me as I sat there ogling the residents' menu. Shepherd's pie and mac and cheese were just two of the dishes that appeared among so many of the other delicious looking things, foods meant to diametrically comfort me and consume me with a biting sense of failure.

Ok. Someone is also better suited than me to prepare meals for my kin.

PEACE OF MIND

Alzheimer's seemed to eat its fill during those two-and-a-half-years my aunt was at Amberwood. Her body went from being bound to a wheelchair to being completely bedridden, her speech went from incoherent to nonexistent.

Alzheimer's seemed to also eat at me.
It started nibbling away at my soul, and
sucking energy from my marrow
until the act of simply showing up became a chore.
I found myself needing a reason to be there,
to reach beyond obligations I felt I owed my aunt;
after all, she could not walk, talk, remember my last visit,
or if I had visited at all.

Would missing a day, a week, or a month, make a difference?

Looking at it this way, made Alzheimer's seem forgiving; that is, until my conscience taunted me with, *haven't seen you here in a while*, and tricked me with self-contempt, suffusing the smiles of Amberwood staffers and causing me to confront my faults in their mirror faces.
Nevertheless, something made me return in spite of myself.
I would drop-in to see if my aunt was clean and comfortable.
I would watch her caregivers buzz 'round and
patients mill about,
while seeking my peace of mind in their existence.

DINNER CONVERSATION

My aunt had been at Amberwood for a month, and during that time she was able to smile but not speak, at least not with words anyone could understand. All the same, I tried my best to talk to her, communicate with her.

"Hey Auntie! Hey, pretty girl."

She would mumble something back, cheerful and incoherent. I'd always respond, albeit self-consciously. I'd abandon myself for a little while pretending to understand what seemed like baby talk, and,

I might have even offered an earnest, "Oh really!."

She was in a reclining wheelchair, an awkward contraption I could push from her room to the dining hall. She had to be spoon fed, something that took loads of patience because she never had an appetite. I'd sit beside her and spoon some food into her mouth and wait, spoon some in and wait, spoon and wait. The process left us with a lot of in-between time that I would fill, talking with the Certified Nursing Assistants. CNAs were also spoon-feeding residents, but occasionally there were residents who fed themselves. One of these residents was Gretchen, a small woman with a serious expression that was just shy of being dour. She sat wide-eyed, eating slowly, mentioning a son who would soon pick her up. She didn't seem rushed, nor did she seem fazed when I said it was raining.

"Raining?" She repeated in a barely detectable accent.

"Yes, pretty hard."

"Rain is güt for my bulbs." Her eyes pointed past the picture window where there were only shrubs, so I imagined she was referring to a garden back home, one with daffodils or tulips or something in which she had taken great pride.

"What color are they?" I asked.

"Yellow."

I pictured them being quite beautiful, thinking, *I could never have bulbs in my garden*. "My dog would dig up bulbs if I had them."

She smiled.

My aunt burbled, and it was as if the three of us were having a dinner conversation. I thought, *funny, possible, but unlikely*. Maybe it was just my aunt passing a little gas.

"Well, Gretchen," I said. "Do you have a dog?"

"My son does."

"Oh really, what kind?"

Gretchen faltered for a moment, trying to find the word, and then she said, "It's a little dog," as if she had recovered the precise answer she had been searching for all along.

"Ah, that's nice. Little dogs are nice."

She looked out the window, perhaps searching through the sheets of rain for a car that might have been her son's. There were several cars parked outside. I turned toward my aunt for another repetition of spoon and wait.

And then Gretchen said again, as if for the first time, "My son is coming to pick me up."

"That's nice." I said, knowing I'd hear her say this again if I sat there long enough. The cars parked outside had been there all morning.

"What kind of car does your son have?"

She seemed to think about this for a while. Her eyes scanned the room as if she was searching for an answer. Her brow furled in a way that made it clear she was lost. So, I redirected.

"We can both look for him."

Just then she brightened. "Blue. My son has a blue car."

I gave her a reassuring nod and said, "He might be stuck in traffic, you know, seeing it's raining as hard as it is."

"He'll be here," she said matter of factly.

She was sure of it, so I hoped that it was true. Gretchen was pleasant company and I appreciated having someone there who could help the time pass a little more quickly. Ten minutes turned into thirty and my aunt finally finished. I excused myself from the table, a little sorry that Gretchen's son had not yet arrived.

"Ok." I said to Gretchen, unlocking the wheel of my aunt's chair. "I have to get Auntie back to her room, but I'll see you soon."

Over the course of the year, I'd made subsequent, but irregular visits to sometimes spoon-feed my aunt in the dining hall. It took patience to feed her when patience was not my thing. Months passed before I saw Gretchen dining again. The disease had advanced to the point she also had to be spoon fed. She was less verbal. Her CNA and I made small talk as we led our respective diners through an orchestration of spoon and wait. And that's when I learned Gretchen had once worked at Amberwood.

"She was thirteen years a CNA."

I let that sink in for a minute before the woman holding the spoon stated the obvious. "Now she's a patient."

"And her son?" I asked, "Does he, I mean did he, visit?"

"Yeah," The woman said, being intentionally vague. But he hadn't come the day it rained, and everything about her tone and demeanor said he hadn't come in a long while. I was afraid to admit the story of Gretchen's son had become my own, one of fewer and fewer visits, and I was embarrassed thinking she might be drawing in her mind my similarities to him.

SPANGLISH WITH MARTA

My aunt had been at Amberwood for almost a year when I'd dropped my visits down to twice monthly. I'd told myself, that this was good enough, the honeymoon was over. I was now a regular and had come to see the Alzheimer's unit with all its flaws and faint, foul smells.

A line of wheelchair occupants was stationed at the entrance. Life for these patients had become something between sad and miserable as they waited for a physical therapy session or a diaper change. I think the facility had placed them there strategically, making them unavoidable, making visitors walk past them to get to the dining area and to the rooms that dotted the walls along each corridor.

Most of these patients were despondent and sat quietly, but a few got quite agitated and loud enough to let everyone know. And then there were the screamers, like the pale woman with white wisps of hair. She was a constant fixture in the line-up who reliably hurled epithets at passersby, and of course one day she gifted me a string of unintelligible words punctuated with an emphatic Black.

I got that she was an Alzheimer's patient like everyone else near the entry, but I was hard pressed to let that one go. It made me wonder if the staff had taken steps to stow her away during tours and open house events. That might have explained why I hadn't encountered her, or her explicatives, earlier. I would simply move past her from that point forward and avoid eye-contact, but it still left me wondering what terrible things had shaped her disposition. Alzheimer's has the tendency to illuminate malice that's already there.

The unmitigated negatives that can come from some Alzheimer's patients is a bit scary. But Alzheimer's can thankfully bring out positives and inhibitions in patients too.

This was the case with a woman named Marta who shuffled up behind me one day and placed her arms around my waist. Marta, with her petite frame and diapered hips that were almost nonexistent. Marta, who looked at me with a pained expression and cried, "¡Ayúdame!"

"What's wrong?" I asked.

"They're gonna get me!"

My first thought was, *Marta has a flair for melodrama*. Her voice teetered in treble before resting upon a withered note. I glanced at the nurse's station, to see if someone would call "Scene!" But nobody did.

Marta was as real as the peril I imagine she had playing out in her head.

She was speaking to me in Spanglish. So, I thought I would respond to her in kind. The CNAs, most of whom spoke Tagalog, communicated with Marta, who was clearly intelligent and obviously a polyglot, with their own hybrid mix of Tagalog, Spanish, and English. The nurse told me a little about Marta who was well traveled. She was originally from Mexico and had immigrated to the U.S. She married a Filipino who took her with him on his overseas travels. I was intrigued as the mystery of overseas missions filled my imagination. The nurse went on to say the two, Marta and her husband, used to work together in some capacity.

"Perhaps they were spies." The nurse turned to me and deadpanned.

I guess I wasn't terribly surprised to learn Amberwood was filled with a cast of characters, many of whom had lived fascinating lives.

The funny and simultaneously not so funny thing about the disease was its indiscriminate nature, its ability to silence the interesting backstories of these patients. So, it could very well have been that Marta's flair for language and melodrama were key to her life and career. At least I kind of liked thinking that. I liked thinking of Marta, full of possibilities even though the thought was bittersweet.

"It's ok, Marta. Cálmate." I patted her arm as she loosened it from my waist. She grabbed my shirttail and continued with me as I pushed my aunt's wheelchair down the corridor.

"Ok." Marta said with another withered note.

"Vamos," I said as I reached my aunt's room with Marta still attached to my behind.

And then without a word of parting she let go, exiting the stage before her drama concluded.

"Bye Marta."

INSIDER INFORMATION

By the second year, I felt I was doing good to visit Amberwood once a month. But on the other hand, there were times I'd binge, coming daily to the facility for a solid week, perhaps wanting to make-up for lost time. Binging was an attempt to make time in the face of never having time.

My aunt was now confined to the bed. She didn't communicate, didn't even mumble and she seldom made eye contact.

I thought I would create a reason to be in her room with her, doing something other than keeping track of the time. So, I installed a bulletin board. I decorated it monthly. In February there were hearts, in March there were shamrocks, etcetera, etcetera. My aunt wasn't able to appreciate it, but I felt compelled to decorate it for myself, or the CNAs, or anyone who happened to pass by her room.

Sometimes I'd read aloud to her on the off chance she could hear me from someplace beyond the void. I wondered if my being there ever made a difference. Maybe it did, but I doubted it.

I doubted myself.

Sara, who was the afternoon CNA, first met me when my aunt used to take meals in the dining hall. Now Auntie got breakfast, lunch, and dinner in bed. I happened to show up for dinner which was served very early in the evening, and the evening was when Sara was about mid-shift.

"Hey Sara, I'll give you a break." She seemed to appreciate that.

I remember thinking it was nice of her to stay and chat with me for a while. Anyone else would have cut and run.

"How you been?"

"Ok."

"Listen. I asked maintenance to get a lift for your aunt's bed. They don't listen to me, but they'll listen to you."

"Huh." I took in what she said. *So, my presence, if nothing else, ensured things got done.* Sara's words urged me to try to be more present, get the low down on Amberwood, and shake things up. "Glad you've told me this, Sara."

"Yeah. Tell 'em to 'fix it.' Tell 'em, and they'll get it done."

"Ok, thanks."

"You bet. I got your back!"

Sara was the one who told me to get a kid-proof lock for the closet when my aunt's clothes went missing, and she told me to place a cassette player high above the closet, away from wandering patients. She offered to play songs on it for my aunt when I was not there, and she told me when the other CNAs wouldn't do the same.

"Pffst," she'd gesture with the sweep of her hand. "They got no patience."

I appreciated having an insider on my side.

LEXI'S SOAPBOX

Each CNA had a unique role, like the guy at the entry, the Bouncer, who directed wandering patients away from the door. He was called when someone got out of hand, when the woman who hurled epithets insulted visitors, and when there was a patient who posed a danger to fellow residents. Although these behaviors were just part of life in the Alzheimer's unit, order still had to be upheld. The CNAs had to tread a fine line between necessary restraint and the potential for broken osteoporotic bones. I trusted the Bouncer was trained to avoid the latter.

Lexi was wheelchair bound, but not like my aunt, because she could push herself around and would sometimes cause a row with other patients. She had a reputation that preceded her, so I knew of her before the two of us had bumped into one another. She scowled at me, but I took it in stride.

"Heya!" I said. "You must be Lexi."

"Heya yourself."

"You ok?"

"I'm sick of folks 'round here and I'm gonna kick some asses." She seemed to exhale these words, measuredly, like smoke from a Marlboro cigarette.

I considered her for a minute thinking *nah, don't get pulled into anything with this troublemaker*. But then she followed me.

"Well?" Lexi pressed me, scooting the wheelchair along with the pads of her feet. She got dangerously close, so I figured she was looking for a co-conspirator.

"Ok," I said with a devilish smile. "What's the plan, Lexi?"

And just like magic, a door opened for Lexi to talk about tools and bustin' out. Her plan seemed to spring from somewhere in her memory had that evaded the editions Alzheimer's famously makes. That's when I found out she had a dog, a horse, and a rifle. Lexi, the old crone, had suddenly become a version of her former and once formidable self. That's when I learned she was a farm girl.

"I don't take shit from nobody." She spat on the carpet. Someone would have to now come clean that up.

I motioned for her to come with. "This way," I said. "The nurse will call the janitor."

Lexi must have needed to get whatever it was, angst and bodily fluids, out of her system.

In that moment, we were thick as thieves. The next time I saw her in the corridor, I better understood her and realized she just needed attention and a soapbox from which she could unload 'whatever.'

And with that, she was good to go.

FAMILY DAY

It wasn't odd to hear a patient screaming in the Alzheimer's unit. My aunt used to scream at one point too. The bizarre sound she made would peak at some primordial pitch and then drop-off. She would lie in bed with her eyes open and wild, and I was afraid she was seeing something terrible: some trauma that Alzheimer's had not yet choked out of her brain.

That's why I didn't think much of it when I heard a patient scream from further down the corridor. I must have winced when her screams turned into curses barked from the back of her throat. Then something broke.

I would unfortunately have to pass her room as it was on the way to the exit. Her door was open. And there was the Bouncer. I met his eyes for a split second, guessing he'd been called to help a nurse who needed to subdue the woman, at least that was the charitable assessment I had given what I saw. It made me think however, *better not to see everything that goes on in a nursing home*. You want to trust the staff is doing what's necessary, and you want them to do what's necessary for the safety of everyone involved: patients, visitors, and CNAs. You don't want to be in the predicament of having to report something, even as the probability of having to do so can hang in the air.

I had no complaints about my aunt's care, save for the occasional dirty diaper; but then she was an "easy" patient: non-ambulatory, non-verbal, and therefore non-combative. I couldn't say that for other patients, some of whom I had seen provoke fights and call names: I understood the potential for violence. Living at home became too dangerous in one way or another for these patients and their families, and a nursing home became one of the safest options for them.

Amberwood offered laundry services, a barber/beauty shop, regularly scheduled activities, family days, religious services, physical therapy, cognitive specialists, a nutritionist, three square meals and snacks, doctors, psychiatrists, nurses, and CNA staff. However, many patients never got to appreciate this full range of services due to the progression of their dementia. That meant that the services were mostly to impress family members and Health inspectors.

I was thankful that my aunt had a quiet room at the back of the Alzheimer's unit. Her window looked out over a beautiful garden. It suited her, this room with a view, but mainly me. I thought it fitting for my aunt who had appreciated her quiet and solitude. She had a beautiful bedroom suite with a north facing bay window when she was at home, and every corner of her room was bathed in light.

I believe Alzheimer's reveals early memories can shape one's experiences and perception. Memories of violence, anger, and trauma beget terrible experiences, while happy memories can affect patient experiences too. When there are circumstances that have left an Alzheimer's patient deeply wounded, I worry that this potentially plays on the psyche in an endless loop.

Personality has its bearing on Alzheimer's too. The disease amplifies aspects of a patient's personality that have always been present. So, you will find that fighters will fight, and not hold back, and lovers will lose their inhibitions.

On family day, things get quite busy. The Alzheimer's unit is staffed with extra CNAs. They are there to engage patients unaccompanied by loved ones. On one of these days, my sons came to visit their aunt. The youngest was a middle schooler, the other a high school freshman; needless to say, they knew how to hold their own. But I briefed them all the same about the wheelchair line-up and its colorful cast of characters.

"Some of the folks might *reproach* you, ignore them. And some folks might *approach* you. Be kind to them. Say 'Hello' if you like, and then move on."

We were walking down the corridor, about to enter the common area, when a withered man stepped from the shadows. He wasn't wearing boxers. Mentally turned off, physically turned on. And just as he was about to remove his shirt, a CNA, flushed and apologetic, spirited him back into his room.

"Huh." I hadn't yet briefed my boys on how Alzheimer's can cause patients to hallucinate: 'hadn't finished that discussion about the birds and the bees. I suppose they'll be better prepared if there's a next time.

My eldest nudged his brother. "Welcome to family day."

SIMPLE GOODBYES

My aunt was on hospice care toward the end and I was exhausted on her behalf. She wouldn't have wanted to go out like this, slowly, and trapped in her own flesh. During the first weeks of hospice, I spent more time than ever before at Amberwood; not because I thought being there would make a difference, but because not being there would be an embarrassment.

There was nothing to do when I was there previously and even less to do with hospice providers floating around. They did the work of the Amberwood staff.

I saw less of Sara and more of the hospice folks—strangers—who were nice, but seemed redundant.

Sans Marta and Lexi's misadventures and my forays into the lives of random Amberwood patients, I found myself lost. The aunt I knew before these final stages of Alzheimer's had long since passed away. I had mourned her and was resisting the act of mourning her again.

I had stepped outside her room where a couple of nurses were at their station looking bored. One was thin but vaguely familiar, I didn't remember her name though; the other was new or had maybe just changed shifts.

"Busy day," I said.

"A little," said the thin one as she took a sip from her thermos.

She looked up at me, her lids half drawn like rolled shades.

"I trust the patients haven't been too much trouble for you today."

The thin nurse looked at the new nurse who shrugged. "We live for trouble."

I chuckled.

A couple of patients passed me, single file. The leader, with a heavy gait, seemed to be inspecting both the carpet and her own slippered feet, padding one and then the other down the corridor. My visits had made me quite the veteran, and as such, I had learned with whom to engage and who to leave alone. I remained silent as the woman passed.

"I haven't seen Gretchen lately."

The neophyte at the nurse's station looked at me curiously.

I repeated the name. "Gretchen. You know, Gretchen with the slight German accent?"

Another patient shuffled by the station. He doubled back.

"Excuse me." His moon shaped face shined up at me. "I think I'm lost because I can't seem to find the hotel exit." He must have known I would help because he'd already cupped my elbow without needing an introduction.

I glanced over my shoulder at the nurse, and she winked at me.

"And you are, Mr..."

"Joe Tanaka. But call me, Joe."

"Where you headed, Joe?"

He launched into a very poignant story, albeit disjointed, about meeting his wife. Joe was clean shaven. So, someone had taken the time to groom him, the barber shop at the facility, or a loved one, maybe.

"I've asked the concierge for help on several occasions," he complained. And then he paused, adding, "I really don't think the service here is worth it."

"Hmm. I understand how that can be frustrating."

Joe's wife was in Japan, according to his story. He had planned to leave the hotel and catch a flight to their rendezvous destination.

"Nice," I said. I tried sounding sincere, improvising my part in the illusion that was, for the moment, very real to Joe. "Well Joe, we'll have to go a little farther, because I think that exit is closed."

By the time we had circled around to the adjacent corridor together, Joe had forgotten where he was going. He rubbed a weathered hand over the back of his grizzled head and thanked me without really knowing what he was thanking me for, and I watched him shuffle back into his room.

"Goodbye, Joe."

EMBRACING PENITENCE

Another shift of nurses had come to work in the Alzheimer's unit. We greeted one another and made small talk.

"Haven't seen Gretchen in a while?" I said casually to one of them. The woman paused and ruefully shook her head, nursing home shorthand or a wordless communication that spoke volumes.

"Bless her."

It hadn't seemed that long since my last tête-à-tête with Gretchen.

Somehow, preoccupied with my own world and my auntie's hospice, I had forgotten this journey is eminently finite and someone's departure can seem abrupt if you miss as little as a day, week, or month.

Time lapsed before I could muster the strength to pay the place another visit.

Lexi was there when I returned. I encountered her scooting down the corridor with the same scowl she'd had the day we first met. She didn't remember me, of course, but I asked how she and her critters were getting along all the same.

"Well," her jaw slack and eyes a bit watery as if I'd opened her book of life, "You know my yella dog? My horse?"

"What's your dog's name again?" I asked, thinking this would perk her up like so many months before. But she dribbled a little about her horse, stuttered, and grappled for words that weren't there.

Sometime between that moment and our last, Alzheimer's had stolen her speech. But I listened, nevertheless, injecting randoms like, "Ya don't say," and "Imagine that."

Maybe she was satisfied, I couldn't be sure, as once again she dug her heels in the carpet and rolled away.

"Good talking with ya, Lexi."

It had grown harder to get a spoon into my aunt's mouth. And it had been impossible to brush her teeth long before that. In fact, her teeth, what was left of them, were clenched shut, no doubt a symptom of the disease? Or perhaps she was by some ungodly force lucid behind those wild and vacant eyes, exerting tension in her jaw, intentionally, with the hope of telling someone she was simply done. Nature's way of converging with her last attempt to exercise some agency.

When my aunt lost her second son to AIDs, she signed an Advance Directive and a DNR (do not resuscitate). I reviewed the latter with the hospice chaplain. The alternative to leaving her unmolested was a feeding tube. I supposed she would have wanted her DNR to apply to feeding now. I supposed I had read a little bit of intent in her clenched teeth, and I shuddered to think that this was my final encounter with the specter of the stylish woman she once was, a woman who made decisions for her children, her household, and herself.

Sara pulled me aside.

"Listen, mija," she said, looking quite earnest. "They don't like me using a spoon to open your aunt's mouth." Sara let me know she had tried her best, feeding my aunt as long as she could. I could hear defeat in her voice. Anything more would have constituted forced feeding.

Sara had gotten my back in ways I could never quantify, but for what it was worth, I managed to save up a little of my thanks and bundle it in an envelope for her to do with as she pleased.

"Thanks Sara. This is for you."

It happened to be that Sara was indeed my intercessor,
forgiving when I went AWOL.

"Is ok. We all get busy."

Picking up conversations as if months hadn't passed.

"Come. See what you aunt ate today."

And gifting me with a smile and absolution after missed holidays.

"Bienvenido."

So, now my aunt is curled up in her bed. Her eyes are open.
They look through me,
hopefully seeing something beautiful on the other side,
something other than my shortcomings.
Hospice calls with status updates every other day now.
We're waiting.

IN MEMORIAM

When my aunt died, I knew I'd traveled to visit her at Amberwood more than I had ever traveled to visit her when she was well and living.

My Amberwood visits surpassed the many times I'd been with her in St. Louis; assumed her immaculate house was my home; played, all those humid summers in her postage stamp yard; attended the obligatory family get-togethers, weddings, births, and funerals; enjoyed the times of laughter, playing the music loud and dancing to Arista's artists on the record player.

It had seemed as if her time at Amberwood had surpassed those many wonderful years she was mother to my cousins who were for a moment the healthy teens fate should have ensured.

These made up what's most memorable about my aunt,
and her life,
and what should be preserved.
So, I've replaced her curled, bedridden figure at Amberwood
with melodramatic Marta,
Lexi, full of spit and vinegar,
Joe, blessed with forgetting his way around the "hotel" and to the exit,
and Gretchen, awaiting her son, and the promise of yellow blossoms.

What Alzheimer's sought to erase, Amberwood retained, in the delightful and sometimes quirky people who roamed its corridors, occupied its rooms, and dreamed of the outdoors.

This is a love letter of sorts for the lives that would have otherwise been simply forgotten.

READING GUIDE

RUMINATIONS ON: A LOVE LETTER

There are explicit ways that love can be expressed, through declaration, touch, food, or simply offering someone help. And there are implicit ways that love can be expressed. Ruminate over some of the *implicit* ways that love might be expressed and list them with their connections to the title and contents of this book.

PROMPT(S):

- What does the author equate to a love letter and why?
- How could similar signs of love, explicit and implicit, be expressed in the form of the written word?
- Do you think color plays a small role in this text? And if yes, explain how?
- What religious iconography or references are present in this text? In what ways do they exist to support the narrative?

- Are technologies changing and/or perhaps broadening the ways in which we signal love?
- How can the things this book euphemistically calls, "love letters," free us? (this references the question, *Uh Huh: But How Do It Free Us?* (1975) by poet and playwright, Sonia Sanchez)
- Can "love letters" address something like the racial wealth gap? Explain how by citing ways and outcomes as you see them.

RUMINATIONS ON CASTE AS A MAJORITY POPULATION AGES

A *Love Letter* intentionally dives into its narrative without explicitly addressing race. The author opens with a description of her aunt, a character that soon recedes in the narrative as her end draws near, allowing other nursing home residents to come into focus. Note the figurative language the author uses to describe her aunt centers on grooming, clothing, and comportment, inferences to class. Whether aspirational or an accurate indication of status, class is a "floating signifier," a term the late sociologist and cultural theorist, Stewart Hall, coined to discuss race. Hall might have agreed race and caste are codependent, operating in the same social structure. Indeed, author Isabelle Wilkerson posits something similar in her book, *Caste: The Origins of Our Discontents.*

PROMPT(S):

- Therefore, discuss how caste informs long-term care communities and similar institutions as people of color will be part of the majority population in the U.S.

- What socio-economic and/or racial and ethnic signifiers do you spot throughout the book? What do they communicate?

- How do contemporary nursing home arrangements belie some of the absurdities of race and caste? How do you see this illustrated in the book?

RUMINATIONS ON THE INDIVIDUAL JUXTAPOSED TO THE INSTITUTION

A *Love Letter* tries to illuminate individuals in every-day situations while writing back to some of the many institutional and systemic problems pervading long-term care and/or healthcare in general.

PROMPT(S):

- Therefore, discuss ways in which institutionalized care might better ensure the dignity of patients with dementia.

- Share your experiences with dementia, with healthcare institutions, or with making long-term care plans with a loved one. If you have not had experiences with any of these, then share how this book inspires conversations around aging, long-term care, advance directives, DNR statements, and other affairs.

- Discuss whether you see comprehensive healthcare/long-term care/and mental health services as a human right. Share your thoughts on how these might be completely reimagined in the U.S.

- Discuss how a reimagined healthcare system could be both an economic and humanitarian win for U.S. inhabitants. Note: the word "citizens" was left out of this discussion regarding healthcare. Why do you think that is?

- What commitment do you think you can make to support changes and/or push for a complete overhaul in healthcare, long-term care, and/or policies as we go forward?

SUPPLEMENTAL READING

Title *Selected Writings on Race and Difference*
Author Stuart Hall
Editors Paul Gilroy, Ruth Wilson Gilmore
Publisher Duke University Press, 2021
ISBN 1478021225, 9781478021223
Length 464 pages
Subjects Social Science ' Black Studies (Global) ' Cultural Criticism

Title *Conversations with Sonia Sanchez*
Author Sonia Sanchez
Editors Joyce Ann Joyce
Publisher Univ. Press of Mississippi, 2007
ISBN 1578069521, 9781578069521
Length 213 pages
Subjects Literary Collections ' American ' African American & Black

Title *Deadly Monopolies*
Author Harriet A. Washington
Publisher Anchor, Reprinted in 2012
ISBN 0767931238, 9780767931236
Length 448 pages
Subjects Medical Ethics ' Patent Law ' African American & Black

Title	*When the Body Says No: The Cost of Hidden Stress*
Author	Gabor Maté
Publisher	Wiley; 1st edition, 2011
ISBN	0470923350, 9780470923351
Length	320 pages
Subjects	Stress and Disease ‘ Alternative Medicine ‘ Self-Help

ACKNOWLEDGMENTS

I started writing late in life and for perhaps slightly different reasons than many of my literary art contemporaries, folk who are young, gifted and much farther along than me, but when I afford myself a little grace, as I am in this moment, I think, *better late than never*, because here is where I begin.

I began, needing to capture some of what I've learned and experienced, some of what I ought to share with my sons and what I ought to shield them from: generational trauma sits at the top of that list. It's the catalyst behind many of the things I didn't get about my mother and my beloved aunts. Despite the buffer of a little time between me, them, and trauma, a shadow remains, clouding some of the things I've tried to do to work through my dubious inheritances before I leave this world. So, I write with an appreciation for my mom and her sisters that I didn't have years ago, and I write to relieve these matriarchs, my muses, from anything that would encumber their deserved rest. Peace be with you.

Ok. Back to my young, gifted, literary art contemporaries, perhaps too many to mention, but I'll try, beginning with those who ushered me through San Jose State University's MFA program.

Thank you, Selena Anderson, my dear professor, thesis director, and mentor; your warm, welcoming way with students and your encouragement sustained me. Thank you, William Armaline; you tossed me a lifeline when I was trying to both form my thesis and a committee; you showed me that writing, worth its effort, turns words into action. And thank you, Keenan Norris, your critiques have been invaluable, your faith in me, empowering, and your willingness to open doors, a game changer. If not for you, I might still be looking for a press like Nomadic and a community with its galaxy of stars to light my literary path: J.K. Fowler, Vernon Keeve III, Daniel B. Summerhill, Tureeda Mikell, Tongo Eisen-Martin, MK Chavez, Laura Salazar, and again, Keenan Norris.

Special thanks to Vernon Keeve III, who we all affectionately call Trey, you've built up my confidence as a new writer with your praise and thoughtful edits, and I'm proud about what will soon hit the press.

And to Vendela Vida, the accomplished author who I'm pleased to say was also my professor, and to Tshaka Campbell, a world-class poet and delightful cosmopolite, thank you. Thank you both for being the bright stars that you are and for generously shining light on my work.

Last, but never in the least, thank you to my sons who give purpose to what I do without even knowing. And thank you to Salah, my best friend and my beloved whose praise I am assured, whether I've produced perfected prose or chicken scratch.

CARMEN KENNEDY

Carmen is quick to recount her good fortune, landing in a MFA program that inspired her to dream, discover, and document her life with some newly acquired knowledge and a smattering of literary alchemy. So accustomed she became to this modus vivendi with its reading, ruminating, and writing, that she planted herself at her alma mater and blossomed quite nicely as a perennial learner and lecturer. You can watch her grow @carmennedy where she posts links to her work, published in the Themis and Acacia journals, and a few of her distinctions, including a James D. Phelan literary award, a Solas Award in the category of culture and ideas, and a little book debuting: 2023.

4 OTHER WAYS TO SUPPORT NOMADIC PRESS WRITERS

Please consider supporting these funds. You can donate on a one-time or monthly basis from $10–∞ You can also more generally support Nomadic Press by donating to our general fund via nomadicpress.org/donate and by continuing to buy our books.

As always, thank you for your support!

Scan the QR code for more information and/or to donate.

You can also donate at nomadicpress.org/store.

ABOUT THE FUNDS

XALAPA FUND

XALAPA FUND

The Xalapa Fund was started in May of 2022 to help offset the airfare costs of Nomadic Press authors to travel to our new retreat space in Xalapa, Veracruz in Mexico. Funds of up to $350 will be dispersed to any Nomadic Press published author who wishes to travel to Xalapa. The funds are kept in a separate bank account and disbursements are overseen by three (3) Nomadic Press authors and Founding Publisher J. K. Fowler.

Inherent in these movements will be cultural exchanges and Nomadic Press will launch a reading series based out of the bookstore/cafe downstairs from the space in August 2022. This series will feature Xalapa-based writers and musicians as well as open-mic slots and will be live streamed to build out relationships between our communities in Oakland, California, Philadelphia, Pennsylvania, and the greater US (and beyond).

EMERGENCY FUND

Right before Labor Day 2020 (and in response to the effects of COVID), Nomadic Press launched its Emergency Fund, a forever fund meant to support Nomadic Press-published writers who have no income, are unemployed, don't qualify for unemployment, have no healthcare, or are just generally in need of covering unexpected or impactful expenses.

Funds are first come, first serve, and are available as long as there is money in the account, and there is a dignity centered internal application that interested folks submit. Disbursements are made for any amount up to $300. All donations made to this fund are kept in a separate account. The Nomadic Press Emergency Fund (NPEF) account and associated processes (like the application) are overseen by Nomadic Press authors and the group meets every month.

BLACK WRITERS FUND

On Juneteenth (June 19) 2020, Nomadic Press launched the Nomadic Press Black Writers Fund (NPBWF), a forever fund that will be directly built into the fabric of our organization for as long as Nomadic Press exists and puts additional monies directly into the pockets of our Black writers at the end of each year.

Here is how it works: $1 of each book sale goes into the fund. At the end of each year, all Nomadic Press authors have the opportunity to voluntarily donate none, part, or all of their royalties to the fund. Anyone from our larger communities can donate to the fund. This is where you come in! At the end of the year, whatever monies are in the fund will be evenly distributed to all Black Nomadic Press authors that have been published by the date of disbursement (mid-to-late December). The fund (and associated, separate bank account) has an oversight team comprised of four authors (Ayodele Nzinga, Daniel B. Summerhill, Dazié Grego-Sykes, and Odelia Younge) + Nomadic Press Executive Director J. K. Fowler.

PAINTING THE STREETS FUND

The Nomadic Press Painting the Streets Fund was launched in February 2022 to support visual arts programs in Oakland flatlands' schools. Its launch coincided with the release of *Painting the Streets: Oakland Uprising in the Time of Rebellion*. Your donations here will go directly into a separate bank account overseen by J. K. Fowler (Nomadic Press), Elena Serrano (Eastside Arts Alliance), Leslie Lopez (EastSide Arts Alliance), Rachel Wolfe-Goldsmith (BAMP), and Andre Jones (BAMP). In addition, all net proceeds from the sale of *Painting the Streets: Oakland Uprising in the Time of Rebellion* will go into this fund. We will share the fund's impact annually on project partner websites. Here are a few schools that we have already earmarked to receive funds: Ile Omode, Madison High School, McClymonds High School, Roosevelt Middle School, Elmhurst Middle School, Castlemont High School, Urban Promise Academy, West Oakland Middle School, and POC Homeschoolers of Oakland.